Flip-a-Quest™!

Do you feel lucky?

If your answer was an immediate, resounding "YES!" then you're ready to play Flip-a-Quest™!

If it was a feeble, "Nah, I'm not lucky at all," then put this book down and go back to doing whatever lame thing you were doing before you picked up this book.

Flip-a-Quest™ is all about luck and fun. Use collectible Flip Disks to decide your journey, or use whatever coin you like to decide your fate. Adventure time can range from ten to thirty minutes based on the luck of your flips. Just follow the easy instructions on each page and you'll know what to do. Each "encounter" is numbered, so you can flip to wherever you need to go by glancing at the top of each page.

Also, you get to keep your character after the adventure's done! You can use your experiences and customizations in each new module!

Have a flippin' good time!

-The Lethcoe Brothers

Lethcoe Brothers games

How to Flip

Position Flip-a-Quest™ Flip Disk or coin on top of your closed fist with thumb tucked under your pointer finger.

Make sure that the edge of one side of the coin sits just over the tip of your thumb.

Flick thumb up launching your collectible Flip Disk into the air! Now you're ready to Flip-a-Quest™!

Draw Your Character

Be sure to include any armor
or weapons that you may
have obtained in previous
Flip-a-Quest™ Adventures!

Bag O' Stuff

Draw any items you've
gained from previous
Flip-a-Quest Adventures!

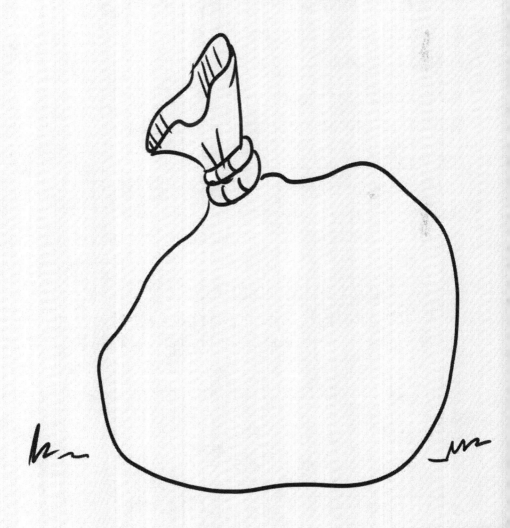

Choose Your Faction!

Align yourself with a Flip Worlds faction. By joining a faction, you will receive special abilities and opportunities in certain encounters. However, you will also suffer consequences in other encounters. Some creatures will have faction alliances as well. Once you have chosen there is no going back. Choose or let fate decide with a flip of your Flip Disk! When you have chosen, seal your decision by using a PEN to write your decision at the bottom of this page!

The Society of the Groovy Moon:

Members of this clan pay homage to the legend of the Groovy Moon. It is said that on July 7, 1967, the moon sneezed. People thought it was so cool that they named it the Groovy Moon.

The Fellowship of the Hippy Tree:

On January, 9, 1970, a curious kid got lost in a forest. He happened upon a magical tree that held out its branches and flung the kid home. The kid could hear the words "FAR OUT!" coming from the tree as he flew.

I swear my allegiance to

_____.

Flip For Your Stats!

Your base stats will be used in different encounters for different purposes. **Flip a Flip Disk or coin for each stat.** Each time it lands on "heads," you get +2 of that ability added to your base stats. If it lands on "tails," you are done with that stat and must move on to the next. Flip as many "heads" as you can in a row to achieve the most points possible! Write the total number in the space next to the ability.

_____ **Muscles:** Used for greater damage in battles and carrying heavy objects.

_____ **Tongue:** Used to charm creatures and get what you want.

_____ **Brains:** Used to accomplish difficult tasks and make stuff.

_____ **Lungs**: Used to increase your overall Life Points.

1. Floss No More!

While sleepily flossing your teeth one morning, a mysterious warlock suddenly appears in the mirror before you!

"Go defeat the mighty dragon Grundmyr," he bellows, "and reclaim the stolen Battle Disk of Power!" He then leans in and begins to whisper with giddy excitement: "The properties of this artifact are coveted beyond imagination. If the holder flips the secret flip sequence, the disk exudes a magical effect that greatly affects the outcome of the battle!" He straightens up, returning to a majestic stance and booming voice. "Seek out the nomadic dwarf Foobis Ironskull in the Moon Mountains. He will help you retrieve this medallion! Here is a map that shows the location of the disk. Now, go get it and bring it back to ME because I really want it."

Flip a Flip Disk or coin.

If it lands on "heads," you jump into a mystic portal that rips open before your eyes.

Turn to encounter 2.

If it lands on "tails," you decide to skip the creepy portal and hail a cab to take you to the Moon Mountains. **Turn to encounter 3.**

2. Kappa!

The portal shoots you out on to some wet grass! You are at the edge of a large pond. "Ah, perfect," you think to yourself, "I'll get hydrated before I track down Foobis!" Just as you reach into the water for a drink, a kappa reaches up and begins to pull you under!

Flip Battle: Flip a Flip Disk or coin several times.

The kappa has 10 Life Points. You have 20 Life Points + your total Lungs points. When either of the fighter's Life Points reaches 0, the battle is over.

If it lands on "heads," you crack some kappa shell for 5 damage + your total Muscles points.

If it lands on "tails," the unnaturally strong hands pull you under for 5 damage!

∽BATTLE STATS∾

MY Life Points:
Heads

OPPONENT'S Life Points:
Tails

| If you win the battle, turn to encounter 4. | If you lose the battle, turn to encounter 5. |

3. Taxi?

Out of nowhere a taxicab comes whirling

around the corner and summons you with a *HONK!*

You scramble over to it, hop in and say, "To the Moon

Mountains! I need to track down Foobis Ironskull!"
The driver speeds away, and before you can say,
"this-must-be-a-bizarre-dream," the passenger-side
door flings open, and you tumble out onto the floor of
a deeply wooded forest. As the cab driver zooms out
of sight, the sounds of the forest begin to come alive.
A sinister cackling can be heard in the distance,
drawing closer by the second.

"Taxi?" you say feebly, but there's no response.

Flip a Flip Disk or coin.
*If it lands on "heads," you scream, "WHERE'S A
PORTAL WHEN YOU NEED ONE!" Just then, a
portal rips open and sucks you in.*
Turn to encounter 6.
*If it lands on "tails," you think, "I know, I'll freeze and
take the form of a scarecrow!"*
Turn to encounter 7.

4. Slappa Kappa!

With a well-placed *CRACK,* you slay the beast!

You receive a kappa shell shield!

Add +2 Lungs!

Draw this on your character!

As you climb out of the bog, you realize that it's quickly getting dark. "I'd better find shelter!" you murmur to yourself. You scan the area and see that there is a small shack in the distance with a lantern hanging above the door. "Friendly!" you think, so you skip over and rap a *bum-bumpa-bump-bump* rhythm on the door, waiting for a kind face to open it. Instead, a loud *BUMP-BUMP* responds from the other side of the door!

Flip a Flip Disk or coin.

If it lands on "heads," you attempt to run away!

Turn to encounter 8.

If it lands on "tails," you yell, "TAXI!" but a mystic portal opens up instead and pulls you in!"

Turn to encounter 6.

5. Pliers Anyone?

You attempt to shake loose the slimy grip the bog dweller has on your shoulders! No good, they're too strong! You reach for anything you might have on you. Yes, the map! You take the map and whack the kappa with it. Bah! That didn't do anything! You scream like a five-year-old girl, hoping *someone* will come to your aid! Lo and behold it works! A hooded dwarf comes bounding over! With a quick *Whoosh* of his axe he slices the kappa's grip, releasing your shoulders!

"Thanks! Who are you?" you inquire.

The dwarf doesn't answer but just utters a long "Hmmm," alluding to his sense of wonder at the situation. He slowly turns a golden ring between his stubby, little fingers.

"Um, I'm looking for someone," you say, interrupting the awkward silence. The dwarf's eyes narrow as he frowns.

Flip a Flip Disk or coin.

If it lands on "heads," you decide to test the dwarf to see if it might be Foobis!

Turn to encounter 10.

If it lands on "tails," you decide to tell the dwarf that you are looking for The Battle Disk of Power!

Turn to encounter 11.

6. Francis!

Feeling like a stretched rubber band, the mystic portal finally spews you out onto a rocky glade. With a simple "pop" the portal disappears.

"Psssst! Over here!" a voice calls out to you from behind some large stones on your left. You look around but see nothing.

"I'm here," squeaks a small voice from the surface of the rock. You spy a tiny, one-horned slug lying stiff as a board!

"Who are you?" you inquire.

"I'm Francis the Unicorn Planking Slug!"

"What the..." you begin to say. Francis just lies there wide-eyed and rigid.

"Quick, be still like me! They're hunting you!"

"I need to find Foobis!" you scream.

"Oooo...Foobis Ironskull," Francis replies. "I know where he is! I'll guide you to him, but first, make like a statue! The Jacks are coming!"

Flip a Flip Disk or coin:

If it lands on "heads," you obey the unicorn planking slug and strike a frozen pose!

Turn to encounter 7.

If it lands on "tails," you grab Francis and take off running, demanding that he tells you where to find Foobis Ironskull!

Turn to encounter 13.

7. Pumpkin Juice!

You freeze in the position of a sulking

scarecrow! Just then, a wandering Jack-O'-Lantern

approaches you.

"Cursed scarecrow!" the creature shrieks and

barfs all over you! The acidy liquid burns your skin!

Flip Battle: Flip a Flip Disk or coin several times.

The Jack-O'-Lantern has 25 Life Points. You have 20 Life Points + your total Lungs Points. When either of the fighter's Life Points reaches 0, the battle is over. If it lands on "heads," you smash the pumpkin for for 5 damage + your total Muscles points. If it lands on "tails," the Jack-O'-Lantern barfs on you for 5 damage!

∾BATTLE STATS∾

MY Life Points:
Heads

OPPONENT'S Life Points:
Tails

If you win the battle, turn to encounter 14.

If you lose the battle, a mystic portal swallows you just before you drown in barf. Turn to encounter 2.

8. For Dryad Out Loud!

You turn around and dash into the woods!

Soon, you are greeted by a little babbling brook.

"Phew, that was scary!" you say, catching your
breath. You bend down to sip some water from the
stream.

"Wasn't it?" a voice says right next to you.

"PSHHHHHHHHHHHHHHH!" You spew water all over the place. "Oh, for cryin' out loud, you scared me!" A friendly-looking dryad is standing next to you.

"You look lost, seeker," she says.

"I'm looking for Foob…" but before you can even finish your sentence, she begins to sing:

> *"Foobis, Foobis, where is Foobis,*
>
> *He is cleverer than the two of us,*
>
> *You be careful on your journey,*
>
> *Take this potion to dodge the gurney!*

You receive a resurrection potion!

If you are about to lose a battle, use this one-time potion to restore all your Life Points!

"Awesome! Can I add you to my friend's list?"

"No."

"Please?"

"No, and if you ask again, I'll take it back."

Turn to encounter 3.

9. Really?

"Oh, hey, Skelinski, lookin' good!" you compliment the creature as you embody the voice and mannerisms of a stand-up comedian. "Yeah, heh, I know you're 'scary' being a skeleton and all. 'Oooooooo...' (you wave your hands next to your head), but you don't scare me. Nope, I can 'see *right through* you! Ha!'" you say feebly while slapping your knee.

"Really," the skeleton replies in a monotone voice, awestruck by the lack of comedic talent you have. The skeleton menacingly moves toward you, bony hands outstretched!

Gravely aware that your humor is unappreciated, you quickly look inside your Bag O' Stuff to see if you have something you can use to help you out of this *deadly* situation!

Flip Decision:

If you have a pair of Gnomish Rocket Boots from a previous Flip-A-Quest adventure, you use them to make a quick exit through a portal up in the sky!

Turn to encounter 6.

If you don't have the Gnomish Rocket Boots, you make a run for it!

Turn to encounter 8.

10. Fanna Fo...

As a test, you break into song, " Ooobis, oobis, bo boobis, banana-fana…," you trail off hoping to lead the dwarf into finishing the song. A long, uncomfortable silence hangs in the air…and… nothing. The dwarf just stares at you. Then, suddenly, the dwarf shouts out, "fo- Foobis!"

"Woot!" you say, jamming your fist in the air! "You know the song!"

"Everyone knows that song," the dwarf replies.

"Yeah, but…" sounding like a balloon slowly losing its air. "I thought that…"

"You thought that I was Foobis?"

"Uh, yeah…well, never mind I guess."

"Ha! I am!" Foobis exclaims. "What do you want from me?"

"I knew it!" you say pointing your finger victoriously. You share your story and the map with Foobis Ironskull. Foobis examines the map.

Flip a Flip Disk or coin:

If you flip "heads," Foobis' eyes widen in shock…

Turn to encounter 11.

If you flip "tails," Foobis knocks you out and steals the map!

Turn to encounter 3.

11. Dun...Dun...Dung!

"Foobis Ironskull is at your service!" the dwarf says with honor. "This map shows that the valued medallion is buried beneath a large pile of dragon dung! See?" the dwarf points his chubby finger at a place on the map called the *Wastelands*.

"That's so gross…and *great*! What an awesome hiding place!" You make a motion to high-five Foobis…and then, looking at his size, you realize it wasn't such a great idea. You make an attempt to quickly change the subject and say," So… how 'bout this great weather we're havin'?" Foobis offended by your insensitivity, looks ready to give you a wallop upside the head!

Flip a Flip Disk or coin.

If it lands on "heads," Foobis yells, "Taxi!" and runs off!

Turn to encounter 3.

If it lands on "tails," you and Ironskull run as fast as you can to the pile of poop!

Turn to encounter 17.

12. Once Upon a Slime

Barely eluding the Jack-O-Lantern, Francis

finally leads you to a petrified giant's head. "Foobis

lives inside that skull," he says, pointing with his eye.

"Aren't you coming?"

"Uh, no, um…see…Foobis…yeah…um, he

doesn't like me very much."

"Whaddya mean?"

"Well, I kinda owe him a golden ring," Francis says sheepishly. "You see, he had this golden ring that he fondly called, 'My Sweetness,' and yeah, I kinda wanted it for myself, so I slipped it off his finger one night and took it. Being a gastropod and all, I'm, well, *sluggish* to say the least; I never had a chance. I'm ashamed of my illicit behavior now, because as he slid it off me, it slipped out of his hand and fell down the drain! He swore if he ever saw me again he'd get out the salt shaker!"

Flip Decision: *If you have the Ring of Traps from a previous Flip-a-Quest adventure, you may choose to give it to Francis as a replacement ring for Foobis.*
Turn to the last page in this book.
If you don't have the Ring of Traps, or decide not to give it up, you walk over to the petrified giant's head.
Turn to encounter 15.

13. Here's Slug in Yer Eye!

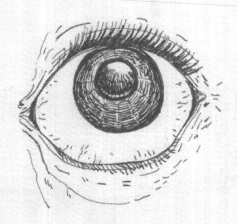

"Look slug, I don't have time for this! Now tell me where Foobis is, or I'll squish you!"

"Oh yeah?" Francis says in a threatening tone. All of the sudden, Francis shoots an enormous amount of slug slime right into your eye!

"My eye!" you scream, dropping him to the ground! Then, Francis stabs you with his horn, causing razor-sharp pain to your big toe!

Flip Battle: Flip a Flip Disk or coin several times.

Francis has 10 Life Points. You have 20 Life Points +

your total Lungs Points. When either of the fighter's

Life Points reaches 0, the battle is over.

If it lands on "heads," you squish Francis for 5

damage + your total Muscles points.

If it lands on "tails," Francis pokes you with his horn

for 5 damage!

✂BATTLE STATS✂

My Life Points:	Opponent's Life Points:
Heads	Tails

If you win the battle, a mystical portal opens up and transports you! Turn to encounter 12.

If you lose the battle, you curl up in a ball and snivel! Turn to encounter 2.

14. Pumpkin Pie!

"Wow, what a crazy creature!" you say with winded breath. As you take a closer look at the goopy remains of the Jack-O'-Lantern, you see that it begins to coalesce into a perfectly formed piece of pumpkin pie!

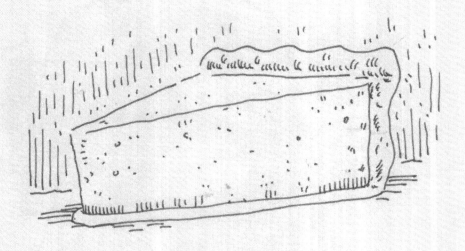

You receive a piece of pumpkin pie!

Put this in your Bag O' Stuff!

As you put the piece of pie in your bag, you wonder why the creature hated scarecrows so much. A moment later, it dawns on you that you haven't eaten anything this whole adventure!

Flip a Flip Disk or Coin.

If it lands on "heads," you decide to eat the Jack-O'-Lantern pie (though as you do, it tastes horrible and you pass out!)

Turn to encounter 3.

If it lands on "tails," you decide you might want to get this piece of pie investigated first before eating it! As you begin walking away, a mystical portal rips open the ground beneath your feet and you fall in!

Turn to encounter 2.

15. Um-Dead?

As you crawl up into the ear canal of the giant's skull, you accidently step on a pile of bones. With a twisting *CRREAAKK*...An undead skeleton suddenly emerges from the ground directly in front of you!

"Holy phalanges!" you scream, attempting to scramble back to the cave entrance .

"Whoa there, you little cutie-patootie," the skeleton says, grabbing your cheek and giving it an extra-hard, endearing squeeze. "Where you runnin' off to in such a hurry? C'mon, I'd love to have your for dinner! How does a nice BBQ steak sound, hmm?"

Flip a Flip Disk or coin.

If it lands on "heads," you say, "Aw shucks, (looking down and sweeping your feet in the dirt) you sure know how to sweet talk 'em!" And then, you spy a dark crevice on your left!

Turn to encounter 16 .

If it lands on "tails," you think it would be a great time to do some improvisational comedy!

Turn to encounter 9.

16. Foobis Ironskull

With lightening reflexes, you fling yourself through a small opening on your left! "Whew, safe!" you shout with glee!

"Eh? Who's there!" echoes a raspy Irish voice from the depths of the cave.

"Foobis? Um, I have a message from a warlock that appeared in my mirror." A hooded, black-bearded dwarf hurries to greet you.

"Ashtooo!" Foobis shouts.

"Gesundheit."

"No, the warlock, his name is Ashtooo!"

"Ashtooo?"

"Gesundheit," says Foobis.

"Thanks!" Wait, what?

"Never mind, what did he tell you?"

"He said you would help me find the Battle Disk of Power." You point to the map. Foobis' eyes narrow.

"The Battle Disk of Power, eh?" "Well, now, retrieving this disk won't be easy. It's under a pile of dragon poop! Foobis points to a dark spot on the map. "We're going to have to battle Grundmyr the dragon for it. How are your battle skills, stranger?"

Flip a Flip Disk or coin.

If it lands on "heads," you say, "Epic! Ever tasted dragon burger?" **Turn to encounter 18.**

If it lands on "tails," Foobis clobber's you and takes the map! **Turn to encounter 3.**

17. Grundmyr!

Arriving at the dung heap, you thrust your hand deep inside the pile of poo! "Wait-for-it… wait…for…it…got it!" You latch onto something and pull! Unfortunately, it was Grundmyr's tail!

Flip Battle: Flip a Flip Disk or coin several times. *Grundmyr has 40 life points. You have 20 Life Points + your total Lungs Points. When either of the fighter's Life Points reaches 0, the battle is over. If it lands on "heads," you deal 5 base damage + your total*

Muscles points.If it lands on "tails," Grundmyr deals 5 damage, slowly turning you into a piece of crispy bacon!

∽BATTLE STATS∽

MY Life PoiNts:
Heads

OPPONENT'S Life PoiNts:
Tails

If you lose the battle, you hear a honking sound in the distance as you fall to the ground. Turn to encounter 3.

If you win the battle, turn to encounter 19.

18. Ah, Poop!

"Off to the heap!" the two of you shout in

unison. After about three hours of trading lame jokes,

your reach your destination. Before you is the biggest

pile of poop you've ever seen, and with it, a creature

that calls this place home! It's a *HUGE zombie* fly!

Flip Battle: Flip a Flip Disk or coin several times.

The zombie fly has 30 Life Points! You have 20 Life Points + your total Lungs Points. If it lands on "heads," you swat the enormous fly for 5 damage + your total Muscles points. If it lands on "tails," the zombie fly infects you for 5 damage!

∽BATTLE STATS∽

MY Life PoiNts:
Heads

OPPONENT'S Life PoiNts:
Tails

If you lose the battle, the zombie juice makes you forget everything. The fly drops you off at a swampy pond.
Turn to encounter 2.

If you win the battle, turn to encounter 20.

19. Ashtooo!

"VICTORY!" you shout, turning around to see if anyone witnessed your awesome fighting skills. Behind you stands a majestic looking warlock.

"Incredible!" Ashtooo says, "you slayed Grundmyr! I see you found Foobis as well, excellent!"

"Yeah, but we still need to get Grundmyr's Disk!" You turn and make a swan dive into the enormous pile of poo.

"WAIT!" Ashtooo warns, but it's too late. You swim around and fling dragon dung everywhere, desperately attempting to finish the mission and retrieve the prize!

"Um, the disk isn't here." says Ashtoo.

You freeze, mouth agape. "What."

"Evidently, it was just a myth."

"You're kidding me."

"Nope, heh, but here, you can have this bucket!"

You receive and epic item!

Ashtooo's Bucket! Holding this bucket adds +2 Muscles to your stats!

The End.

(Proceed to the Draw Your Character page.)

20. Battle Disk of Power!

"Poopsie?" you hear something say in a voice that sounds like a mix between someone gargling Jell-O and nails scraping a chalkboard. "Poopsie, are you alive?" A gigantic, sapphire blue dragon erupts from a cavern behind the pile of dung. "YOU!" the dragon growls, "You killed POOPSIE!"

"I...I...didn't mean..." you stutter.

"THANK YOU so much! Hooooooo nelly, she was a pesky fly! Now, I bet you'd like to have the Battle Disk of Power as a reward wouldn't you?"

"Yes!" you exclaim.

"Ha, that's funny. No-can-do, but I'll infuse your Flip Disk with power for your efforts."

You receive an epic enchantment!

Spirit of Grundmyr!

Your Flip Disk is infused with power! Add +2 Brains to your stats!

The End.

(Proceed to the Draw Yourself page!)

Draw Your Character!

Make sure you add your magic items to your character!

Create a Map of Your Adventure!

Draw your path of encounters!

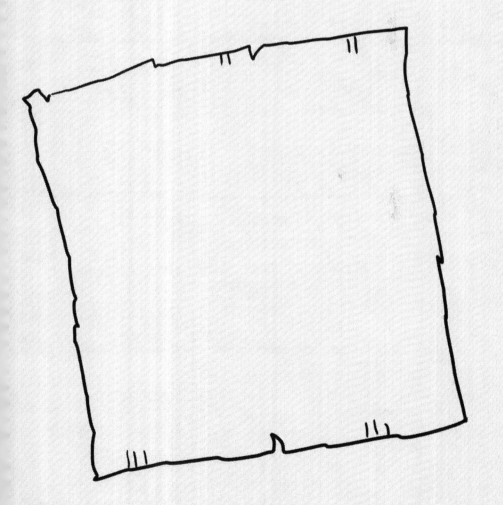

Make a Comic That Brags of Your Mighty Heroics!

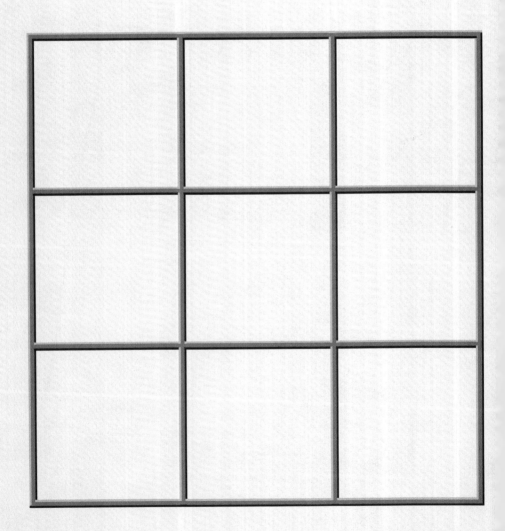

Notes and Doodles

Battle Disks!

Take the adventure outside of the book by battling your friends with official Flip-a-Quest™ Battle Disks! Each Battle Disk has a "heads" and a "tails" side. The "heads" side has Life Points. The "tails" side has Damage Points. Battle Disks also work as Flip Disks for adventure module play! Collect them all!

(Officially sanctioned Battle Events rank players on the lethcoebrothersgames.com website. See website for details and event listings.)

Here's How to Play:

1. Players face each other and flip their Battle Disks!

2. If they both land on matching sides, players re-flip!

3. If they land on opposite sides, the player who lands on *Damage,* deals damage to the opposing players *Life Points*!

4. A player wins by getting the opponent's Life Points down to zero and is awarded the opponent's Battle Disk as a prize!

Coming Soon!

More excitement to be found in

the next Flip-a-Quest™ Module!

Be sure to check flipaquest.com

for official collectible Flip-a-

Quest™ Battle Disks and

Adventure Module updates!

Flip-a-Quest™ is a product of Lethcoe Brothers games.

Lethcoe Brothers games

Real Games for Real People.

(Secret Page!)

WARNING:

(This page is to be read <u>only</u> if you gave the Ring of Traps to Francis during encounter 12.)

Congratulations, faithful adventurer! You have been led to the secret page! Only those who chose to give up the Ring of Traps can access this page! Giving up the ring was not an easy decision, but no risk, no reward, *right*?

So, here's how the story played out:

You said, "Hey Fran, I have a ring! Why don't you take it and give it to Foobis to redeem yourself?"

Francis said, "Cool, man, I'll do that!" So Francis slinked into the cave and said, "Hey Foo, I got you a replace…," (but he didn't get to finish his sentence because a huge salt shaker poured salt on him and he shriveled up. Yeah, sad, I know. *BUT*, there's more!)

Foobis, seeing something glittering on Francis' shriveled corpse, said, "Ooooooooooo, wait a minute, what is this? My Sweetness? Is that you? OH, JOY! YOU'VE RETURNED TO ME!" He then looked down at Francis and tried to save him by pouring water on him, but no luck. Foobis then ran out of his cave and saw you there. Since he felt so bad about killing the only unicorn planking slug ever to exist, he decided to give you a prize instead!

Foobis Ironskull gives you
MY SWEETNESS!

(Add +5 Tongue and +5 Lungs to your stats!)

Turn to encounter 15.

Made in the USA
Lexington, KY
08 December 2013